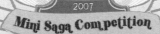

2007

Mini Saga Competition

Young Writers

in association with

STAEDTLER

mini
S·A·G·A·S·

Co Durham

First published in Great Britain in 2007 by
Young Writers, Remus House, Coltsfoot Drive,
Peterborough, PE2 9JX
Tel (01733) 890066 Fax (01733) 313524
All Rights Reserved

Disclaimer
Young Writers has maintained every effort
to publish stories that will not cause offence.
Any stories, events or activities relating to individuals
should be read as fictional pieces and not construed
as real-life character portrayal.

Foreword

Young Writers was established in 1991, with the aim of encouraging the children and young adults of today to think and write creatively. Our latest secondary school competition, 'Mini S.A.G.A.S.', posed an exciting challenge for these young authors: to write, in no more than fifty words, a story encompassing a beginning, a middle and an end.
We call this the mini saga.

Mini S.A.G.A.S. Co Durham is our latest offering from the wealth of young talent that has mastered this incredibly challenging form. With such an abundance of imagination, humour and ability evident in such a wide variety of stories, these young writers cannot fail to enthral and excite with every tale.

Contents

St Bede's RC Comprehensive School, Peterlee

St Leonard's RC Comprehensive School, Durham

Spennymoor Comprehensive School

The Mini Sagas

Ride Of My Life!

The sun blinded me as I slowly went up and up. As we got to the top we flew over the edge. Tears streamed down my face. I went from side to side. I almost came out of my seat then we came to a sudden stop. It was over!

Jasmin Parker (12)
Hummersknott School & Language College

13

Morbid Me

Down the path I heard something - a bird. Then something in the woods - a small rat. Then to the right of me … temptation. Then I woke from my horrible dream and something inside of me stopped - my heart. I had died. There was no one to mourn my grave.

Andrew Grainger (15)
Hummersknott School & Language College

14

Action!

I walked over to what I thought was a drama event. People gathered to see what looked like a horrific murder scene. An outline stained on the floor resembling the outline of someone lying with no will to live. My stomach twisted into a knot … when someone shouted, 'Action!'

Amy Petty (15)
Hummersknott School & Language College

15

What A Relief!

The wind screamed on my face as paper blew around the room, a continuous gale of wind disrupting everything. Work completely stopped for a minute, everyone shocked at the sudden blast of freezing air. I shivered fiercely then flicked a switch. The fan ground to a halt. What a relief!

Emma Whitfield (15)
Hummersknott School & Language College

16

Ten Thousand Dollars

The green was left there, out in the open, in the seductive streets of New York, only to be taken by an intimate stranger. He took his winnings and made an escape. On his drastic departure he checked the mysterious content of his package. Inside it he found Coke Zero.

Tom Lewis (15)
Hummersknott School & Language College

17

Splash!

The water trickles down the mountainside as blue as the sky. I bend down to take a drink and suddenly, *splash!* My silly little brother throws a rock right next to me and splashes me all over so I get really wet. I am really going to get him back.

Hannah Straughan (12)
Hummersknott School & Language College

Alone?

The door slammed shut. She was in complete darkness. There was no one there. She turned around to leave again but the door was locked. She shouted. It was no use. She was in a house in the middle of nowhere. She turned around and saw a figure. She screamed.

Erin Smith (14)
St Bede's Catholic School & Sixth Form College, Lanchester

The Long, Dark Tunnel

'Wait!' cried Carol, her voice echoing down the long, dark tunnel. She could just see Fred's figure silhouetted against the moonlight that seeped through the gap at the end of the tunnel. He mustn't have been able to hear her ... seconds after, he disappeared out into the cold ...

Stevie Howe (14)

St Bede's Catholic School & Sixth Form College, Lanchester

A Fright In The Night

The wind blew the door wide open. Sally sat up as the door started to creak. 'It's just the door,' she said, trying to calm herself down. She started to doze off when she heard a screeching sound. 'What's that?' She went to the window to see what it was …

Emily Davison (14)

St Bede's Catholic School & Sixth Form College, Lanchester

The Cliff

'Stop, please!' yelled Emma. This was it, the end of her life. Her whole life flashed before her eyes. She slammed the brakes as hard as she could. The edge of the cliff was coming closer and closer. She closed her eyes tightly and held on to the steering wheel …

Victoria Wilson (14)
St Bede's Catholic School & Sixth Form College, Lanchester

22

Don't Look Behind You

Not soon after entering the graveyard she heard the footsteps behind her. The faster she walked the closer and louder they got. A sense of someone breathing down her back … a hand on her shoulder then she felt it - something sharp on her neck. Her heart stopped.

Jade Glass (14)
St Bede's Catholic School & Sixth Form College, Lanchester

The Blinding Pain

The gang were closing in. I could not see for the pain.
I didn't know what was happening. All I knew was
pain as they lashed me again with the whip. The pain
was unbearable. I could feel my head being battered
against the wall. The lights shut off ... gone.

Damien Gorman (14)
St Bede's Catholic School & Sixth Form College, Lanchester

No Mercy

The stage, set. Troops encircled the darkness surrounding their feeble souls. Shots fired, babies cried. North Korea … no questions asked. Love was gone, peace too. The flag, once white and pure, had been tarnished with unnecessary bloodshed. The stage, set … troops encircled the darkness. Darkness swallowed them whole. No mercy.

Kieran Dodds (14)
St Bede's Catholic School & Sixth Form College, Lanchester

25

What's That?

Boom! Crash! Bang! What's that? I turned around. The door creaked, lights out. A chilling scream. I ran, lost in darkness, footsteps behind me. Bats flew at me. I reached for the door - locked. A bony hand grabbed my arm. I screamed but it was alone. No one heard me.

Catherine Gardiner (14)
St Bede's Catholic School & Sixth Form College, Lanchester

The Dream

The doors opened. I flounced gracefully through in my exquisite dress. Everyone looked at how glamorous I was. Elegantly I walked into the room. A charming man asked me to dance. The diamonds on my dress glistened as I twirled around in sheer bliss … shame it was all a dream.

Amy Sinclair (14)
St Bede's Catholic School & Sixth Form College, Lanchester

27

Untitled

Rossi losing, Johnson winning. Come on Rossi, take
him, take him.
'Last lap,' calls the radio. 'Last corner.'
He does it, takes him! Rossi first, Johnson second.
My wish comes true. He takes the title Moto GP
Champion for the first time in two years … he's back
from the bottom!

Harvey Skinner (12)
St Bede's Catholic School & Sixth Form College, Lanchester

My Ghostly Dad

I stumbled constantly down the dark alley, step by step. There was an evil presence in the bitter cold wind. The wind changed also as if it was running away. My heart was beating uncontrollably. My hands were trembling too. As it was getting closer, I had flashbacks of … Dad.

Daniel Rooney (12)
St Bede's Catholic School & Sixth Form College, Lanchester

29

Going Out Of The House

I woke up, opened my curtains. The sun was shining.
I raced downstairs and ate my scrumptious fulfilling
breakfast. Then threw my clothes on, my face was
gleaming. I was so excited. I couldn't wait. Mum
drove the car very fast but when we got there the
gates were locked.

Ashleigh Rutherford-McDougal (12)
St Bede's Catholic School & Sixth Form College, Lanchester

The False Cry For Help

As I climbed the stairs he hobbled down asking for help. I carried his crutches while he held the handrail. He stumbled often, steadying himself on my arm. Reaching the bottom eventually, thanking me, we parted. I felt great until someone asked me for the time. Where was my watch?

Philip Nixon (12)
St Bede's Catholic School & Sixth Form College, Lanchester

The Game

Sitting on my own watching the game, watching United drawing again, wishing I was on with Rooney. Giggsy misses, Owen scores, 1-0 Liverpool. Then the moment comes - I'm on. Here I am, on the pitch. I shoot, I score. I score the all-important FA Cup super winning goal.

Connor Dixon (12)

St Bede's Catholic School & Sixth Form College, Lanchester

School Prom

One night after school the Year Elevens had a prom.
They had a prom to celebrate how well they'd
worked. My sister went to see her friend's prom
dress, it was gorgeous. When my sister's friend put
on her dress the zip got stuck and it ripped. What a
disaster.

Abbie Spence (11)
St Bede's Catholic School & Sixth Form College, Lanchester

33

My Best Friend Jim

I am so sad that my best friend Jim died last night. We gave him a good send-off into Heaven. We made him a gravestone and made him a coffin. It did not cost anything because he was my pet goldfish who was four years old today.

Liam Hughes (11)
St Bede's Catholic School & Sixth Form College, Lanchester

Save Me

There they were coming up to me … they were annoyed.
'I told you the consequences.'
'It's got nothing to do with me anymore,' I said.
They were silent. 'I have nothing of value. I can't do anything.'
Suddenly I heard gunshots. 'You're here, save me!'
'I can't,' he whispered mysteriously.

Eoin Stephenson (12)
St Bede's Catholic School & Sixth Form College, Lanchester

Ahh, Cute!

We went to visit the cats at the RSPCA. Cute! We fell in love with kitten Grace straight away. Cute! So we took Grace home to get her settled in. After the first week she started to get used to us. Two weeks later the cat had kittens. Bless them.

Emily Peacock (12)
St Bede's Catholic School & Sixth Form College, Lanchester

Waterfall Treasure

A little boy was told there was treasure in the waterfall. But there was no treasure; some teenager had made it up. But the child found a door. He opened it and he saw a big cup of gold. He took it - the ground shook. He escaped the cave, luckily.

Michael Dougherty (12)
St Bede's Catholic School & Sixth Form College, Lanchester

37

Red Eyes

I walked along the dark path and heard rustling in the
bushes and trees. Suddenly I saw big red eyes coming
towards me, they got so close I screamed and ran
as fast as I could. I turned around and went into the
light to find … it was my *dog!*

Abigail Barnes (13)
St Bede's Catholic School & Sixth Form College, Lanchester

Hunters

They went hunting, chasing lions for meat and fur. They saw one - fiercely it turned round and ran towards them. They ran away. They went back - the lion ran away. They chased it, they then wrestled it to the ground. It bit them. A man came and killed the hunters.

Jake Miller (12)

St Bede's Catholic School & Sixth Form College, Lanchester

39

Fear

Bang! What was that? Who was that? Why were they
doing it?
'Maybe it was a murder,' whispered Mark.
'Shut it Mark,' shouted Sarah.
'With a gun,' laughed Mark.
'Yeah, well let's look.'
As the friends crept into the wood the banging got
louder; all they could do was scream.

Daisy Walton (11)
St Bede's Catholic School & Sixth Form College, Lanchester

Waiting For The Summer

I sat on the blissful sand staring out at the horizon.
The sun shone in the baby-blue sky and my feet sank
in the hot sand as I gazed at the shimmering ocean.
But reality soon returned, and I sat in Spanish waiting
for those long weeks to end.

Abigail Shield (12)
St Bede's Catholic School & Sixth Form College, Lanchester

Late Again

'Run, run Ross, run,' Tasha screamed.
Ross was running down the path. A bright light
beamed down on him. He screamed, 'The aliens
have landed.'
Tash laughed, 'It is my torch you idiot.
They ran home as it was past Ross' 7 o'clock bedtime
story.

Meagan Clarke (14)
St Bede's Catholic School & Sixth Form College, Lanchester

Wet

One time, in the park, when I had the dog, a person threw a ball in the river and the dog chased after it and jumped into the river. Sadly I was attached to the lead; the dog pulled me into the river and I got very wet!

Adam Joyce (13)

St Bede's Catholic School & Sixth Form College, Lanchester

43

Broken Leg

I was playing out on a sunny hot day. Me and my friends were playing in the boring street. We were playing tacky football. Someone got injured. He was a boy called Jordan. He was very strong. My mum rang the hospital. He had a broken leg.

Reece Driver (12)

St Bede's Catholic School & Sixth Form College, Lanchester

Greed

Biscuits were going quicker and quicker.
'Oh Dad!'
The crisp cupboard was empty.
'Oh Dad!'
The jam had gone Mam bought this morning.
'Oh Dad!'
While Mam yelled at Dad, I went upstairs to find my
baby brother Ben with a pot of jam.
Oh my baby brother Ben! (Greedy!)

Charlotte Watson (12)
St Bede's Catholic School & Sixth Form College, Lanchester

The Murder At Midnight

There was an old man strolling along Old Kent Road. After an hour he saw a dark creepy shadow coming towards him, preventing him to walk any further. It said, 'Follow the road at midnight. You will find me strolling.' So he followed it and found bullets going through himself.

Paul Gardiner (12)
St Bede's Catholic School & Sixth Form College, Lanchester

Untitled

Last Sunday I went out on my bike to see my friend because we were going on a bike ride. We got halfway through and I got a flat tyre so I had to push my bike all the way back home and my dad told me off. Ooh!

Andrew Breen (13)
St Bede's Catholic School & Sixth Form College, Lanchester

Who Dares Wins

I hear *thud, thud, thud* as he storms up the stairs. I lie frightened under my bed. I hear the door creak open and feel the floor bounce as he comes towards me. As sweat runs down my face he shouts, 'Okay, come out, you win.' …
It's hide-and-seek!

Jamie Haff (14)

St Bede's Catholic School & Sixth Form College, Lanchester

One Dark Night

It was dark and I was walking. He was behind me; I
was scared. The footsteps behind me were getting
louder and louder. I heard him breathing deeply. I
started walking faster. Suddenly my brother grabbed
me and murmured, 'I got you!'
I was on. It was hide-and-seek.

Danielle Batty (13)
St Bede's Catholic School & Sixth Form College, Lanchester

Hobos

Just another hobo kicked onto the street. A couple of hobos I happened to meet. A few beers later we staggered about. We walked into a wall, we all got knocked out. As I awoke the following morning, bruises on my head, unlike my fellow hobos, they were all dead.

Alexander Harrison (12)
St Bede's Catholic School & Sixth Form College, Lanchester

At The Edge

Stopping for a second or two, waiting to drop
down. My heart beats fast and butterflies flop in my
churning stomach. As three rows of eight are filled I
wait for the sudden drop. I hear people screaming. A
drop approaches. It eventually finishes, people get off
'Sheikra' the ride.

Rebecca Murphy (12)
St Bede's Catholic School & Sixth Form College, Lanchester

A New Beginning

Here I am. I hope I don't die, I'm petrified. This is one of the worst days of my life. Oh no someone tall's approaching.

'Lost?' I nod silently. 'Scared?' I nod. She smiles; that makes me realise everything's going to be okay at my first day of primary school.

Paige Kennedy (11)
St Bede's Catholic School & Sixth Form College, Lanchester

The Disturbed Sleep

I was drifting off to sleep. The front door banged, followed by a gunshot. My whole body shook with terror. A loud shout came from nowhere. Sweat dripped from me. The letterbox creaked. I thought I was in great danger ... but it was the television and the postman.

Michael Cain (14)
St Bede's Catholic School & Sixth Form College, Lanchester

En Route

I dropped three thousand feet in the air. I felt butterflies in my stomach; I thought I was going to die in mid-air; my heart was racing. The plane eventually came to a halt on the runway. I was in Florida, my holiday home - sun, sand, solitude, space, sea!

Kevin Denman (13)
St Bede's Catholic School & Sixth Form College, Lanchester

Going To School

I got up one morning, struggling to get out of bed.
I was running downstairs to get my breakfast,
watching time tick by. I rushed upstairs to put my
clothes on, went out the door, got on the bus, got off
at school … and realised it was Saturday!

Nicole Allison (14)
St Bede's Catholic School & Sixth Form College, Lanchester

Coast To Coast

We were doing the coast to coast on our bikes. We had reached Waskerly Café. We started to speed up when Jamie's handlebar hit mine and we were skidding uncontrollably along the gravel. Jack and Naomi stood there laughing.

Ashleigh Lister (14)
St Bede's Catholic School & Sixth Form College, Lanchester

Bang, Bang, You Shot Her Down!

There Cassie was, standing, waiting. Every noise could be the last thing she heard. She dared not scream - he might hear her. Then she heard him and she braced herself. He opened the cupboard door. He took something out his pocket. *Click! Bang! Thud!* Cassie dropped to the floor dead!

Zóe Logan-McCance (14)
St Bede's Catholic School & Sixth Form College, Lanchester

Waiting

He stood there waiting for her, watching every move of anything that came close to him. She came closer to him, walking in the darkness. She got him and looked him straight in the eye, her beautiful big blue eyes staring at him. Her only words were, 'It's over.'

Stephen Smith (14)
St Bede's Catholic School & Sixth Form College, Lanchester

Fflorence

She looks in the mirror and watches herself take chunks of skin out of her face and wrists, seeing the blood drip off her body onto the bathroom tiles. She starts to scream. Her mother runs up the stairs and starts banging on the door.
She finally gets in. Death.

Shannon Glendinning (12)
St Bede's Catholic School & Sixth Form College, Lanchester

The House

I travelled to the house, a remote ruined house. I walked in only to find that it wasn't empty after all. I saw a man up the hall. He approached. The door slammed behind me. He still came. He grabbed me, then stabbed me … looks like the stories were true.

Jack Kearney (13)
St Bede's Catholic School & Sixth Form College, Lanchester

Is It Her?

There I was arguing away with her. She got mad and
stormed out the house. She was wearing a bright
orange coat. I was looking for hours in the woods,
then I saw her. I went over and said, 'Let's go home.'
… But was it her?

Cameron Coates (13)
St Bede's Catholic School & Sixth Form College, Lanchester

Fire!

Flames roaring, I hid under the table, screaming and shouting, fire blazing. I edged back and back, trying to escape the frightful flames. I felt hot fire burning my skin. I heard sirens, fire engines and ambulances. White lights all around me. They're too late. I have left this Earth.

Sarah McNestry (12)
St Bede's Catholic School & Sixth Form College, Lanchester

The Lonely Soul

Flames burning, voices screaming, tears falling down
my face like a rainstorm. Now I'm alone; abandoned
by my father and my mother killed. 'But she was not
a witch!' I scream at the top of my voice. 'You are all
cold-blooded murderers.'
They all laughed - I cried.

Melissa Lewins (13)
St Bede's Catholic School & Sixth Form College, Lanchester

63

Engulfed In Darkness

Breath partly filling my trapped lungs, I struggle for every breath. Turning my head to the right I see my husband on the ground, launched headfirst out of the windshield. He had no chance of surviving. Slowly starting to fade … I watch my love being dragged off into darkness.

Charlotte Huff (13)
St Bede's Catholic School & Sixth Form College, Lanchester

Kick Of The Game

Extra time began. Rooney powered through the players until a defender slid him from behind. He won a free kick. Beckham hit the ball through the air. It soared like a bird and crashed into the back of the net. The crowd chanted, 'Goal! Goal!' The World Cup was won.

Joseph Reed (13)
St Bede's Catholic School & Sixth Form College, Lanchester

The Crash

I cannot remember what happened. I can only think about a massive bang and the airbag hitting my bruised face … I now find myself in a room as white as snow, full of emptiness. I can hear doctors shouting, 'Come on, come on!' I look down at myself …

Thomas Nearney (13)
St Bede's Catholic School & Sixth Form College, Lanchester

Hammer Of Blood

The shrill screams of her best friend made Nat's heart pound like a machine gun. She was in big trouble. Racing through to the kitchen, Nat could still hear Emily's screams. Nat surprised herself as she started to cry. She washed the blood off the hammer which just killed Emily!

David Hopper (13)

St Bede's Catholic School & Sixth Form College, Lanchester

The Morning Panic

I was walking along the street and then I saw it. It was big and red. I was scared; I started to run fast. I got faster and faster. I got so fast I was nearly tripping over my feet … and then I caught the school bus - lucky for me.

James Patterson (13)
St Bede's Catholic School & Sixth Form College, Lanchester

Across The Field

I was walking across the field over the road from my house, when something black ran past me and disappeared into the grass. I soon got bored and threw a stick. Suddenly something jumped up and caught it and disappeared again. I looked closer … and realised it was my dog.

Lucy-Kate Affum (12)
St Bede's Catholic School & Sixth Form College, Lanchester

What?

'What?' I said to my mum in horror. I asked my mum to say the dreaded words again.

My mum repeated herself once again. 'Your cousin John is coming to stay. He's travelling over today.' Then suddenly the doorbell rang. It was John. 'He's early,' Mum said.

Oh no!

Shaun Malpass (12)

St Bede's Catholic School & Sixth Form College, Lanchester

All Alone

Nobody likes him. He drowns in the noise of the
school. People's words do more damage than they
could realise. In a dark place he weeps. Funny,
he doesn't hate individuals, but people in general.
Register - he's last.
'Dakman, Oliver?'
'Present.'
'Niklas, Hans?'
'Present.'
'Hitler, Adolf?'
He mumbles sadly.

Conor Robinson (14)
St Bede's Catholic School & Sixth Form College, Lanchester

71

Untitled

As we fell through the air the wind hit our faces; our eyes watered. I glanced at Uncle Harry, his eyes twinkled. 'Slow down,' I screamed. The red plane's wing tilted. *Bang!* We were surrounded by a cloud of thick black smoke. 'What was that?' I shouted in curiosity.

Daniel Appleby (13)
St Bede's Catholic School & Sixth Form College, Lanchester

The Show I Died For

The crowd were roaring like an angry bull, all waiting to see my show. My friends and I were standing upon the stage in the courtyard of the emperor's castle. The crowd went silent - now is the time … the floor dropped, the rope tightened, my neck snapped. I stopped moving.

Iain Keenan (13)
St Bede's Catholic School & Sixth Form College, Lanchester

Space

Travelling through the solar system, going here and there, we travelled from planet to planet and also to the sun. As we approached the fire the lights went red, for we all knew what this meant. Everybody ran, stampeding like a bull. Everything went quiet and the sun went *bang!*

Jacob Cain (11)
St Bede's Catholic School & Sixth Form College, Lanchester

Ouch!

I jumped out of the plane but all was not well - my parachute was not working. It had been sabotaged. Who could have done this? I know of no one who would do this to me. I felt the wind on my face as I smacked into the hard ground.

Grant Ridley (12)
St Bede's Catholic School & Sixth Form College, Lanchester

The Road To Wembley

I was playing for Newcastle United and it was the semi-final against Sunderland … we won 6-nil. Then we went to the new Wembley against Manchester United and we won 3-nil. We were jumping around and drinking alcohol out of the trophy. It was the best match.

Bradley Fairhurst (11)
St Bede's Catholic School & Sixth Form College, Lanchester

The Runaway

It was early in the morning before my mum and dad were awake. I called my friend and said, 'Got the tickets?'

'Yes.'

'Hell, let's go.'

We were at the train station and I finally found Brad so we got on the train and set off to London.

'The key!'

David Cross (12)

St Bede's Catholic School & Sixth Form College, Lanchester

77

Jack And Jill

Jack and Jill were a brother and sister who decided to climb an extremely tall mountain. They reached the top and slipped down the middle. The mountain turned out to be a bubbling volcano. It suddenly erupted and that was the end of Jack and Jill.

Maxine Hamflett (14)
St Bede's Catholic School & Sixth Form College, Lanchester

My Death

I carefully strolled, watching every step for sticks that snapped or booby traps. I was alone … that's what Vietnam's like. The distant sound of gunfire came closer. I looked through the dense jungle. A sudden flash from a bush seemed to bring pain to me. Dead, on my last tour.

Ryan Laddie (13)
St Bede's Catholic School & Sixth Form College, Lanchester

The World In Mourning

I woke, startled, confused. How had I got here?
Car crash! What? When?
'It was yesterday,' I was told.
My leg is in a cast. My head aches. The only survivor -
ten people dead. Made headlines on the news. How
could something so severe happen? The whole world
mourns.

Peter Westgarth (14)
St Bede's Catholic School & Sixth Form College, Lanchester

Nam 68

Raise my rifle. Aim for his head, canopy blocks my shot, bayonet attacks. Panic floods through me, adrenaline does too. First fight at 19 years old. I thrust forward, catch his throat, blood everywhere. He slumps down, I cheer but there's more. Look about. Spot another … raise my rifle …

Christopher Affum (14)
St Bede's Catholic School & Sixth Form College, Lanchester

My Journey To Space

Sitting upright, hair blown back against the seat.
Tears slowly dripping down my face as the crackling
sound of the rocket soars through space like a bird in
the sky. The blinding twinkle of stars, the chill of the
night sky. Have I arrived in space?

Ashleigh Taylor (14)
St Bede's Catholic School & Sixth Form College, Lanchester

Where Is She?

There I sat, waiting, everyone met their parents with smiles on their faces. There I was, still waiting, all the children going home, happily. Then there was me, waiting, I knew she wouldn't be long but where was she? What was so important that I should be kept waiting?

Karyn Maughan (14)
St Bede's Catholic School & Sixth Form College, Lanchester

Roaring Flames

It burned bright, blazing orange.
She screamed; blistering heat all around as the thick
smoke rose.
She coughed; crackling and roaring in the doorway.
She cried out; destroying everything in its path. She
hid; spreading rapidly from room to room.
She wept; it was too late … she was trapped!

Elise Waller (12)
St Bede's Catholic School & Sixth Form College, Lanchester

84

Below The Line

Standing in a line, dominated by tall figures. I stood hiding my eyes behind my stringy hair in embarrassment. My blood pumping like water boiling in a kettle. One more step then I will be judged, the thick black line was above me I did not reach the height requirement.

Danielle Barron (13)
St Bede's Catholic School & Sixth Form College, Lanchester

Running

I'm running, desperate to get home. My house
seems to be getting further away. The man's pace of
running's getting quicker. He is shouting, 'I'll get you!'
I run like a cheetah chasing after its prey. I cross the
road and then … you can guess where I am now …
Heaven!

Francesca Loughran (13)
St Bede's Catholic School & Sixth Form College, Lanchester

Lost

Running through the forest as fast as I could, my brother followed me in the hope I could find the way out. We were lost in the woods! Just went out for a picnic. Now lost and terrified. There was light that we saw … we were free again.

Katharina Effiot (13)
St Bede's Catholic School & Sixth Form College, Lanchester

Lost And Found

I was lost. When I turned Mum had left. I started to get frightened walking up and down the aisles. Lots of people staring, sweat dripping from me. I didn't want to cry. A woman asked me something but I kept walking. Mum came around the corner. I was found.

Hayley Blight (12)
St Bede's Catholic School & Sixth Form College, Lanchester

The Pig That Lost His Oink!

I went into the barn and there stood a tiny piglet, the rest were squealing out, but this one didn't make a noise. It hasn't squealed all of its life. It hasn't even given a little weep. Now it is getting old, the hope for the piglet has gone forever.

Rebecca Wright (13)
St Bede's Catholic School & Sixth Form College, Lanchester

Little Maddie

I was sitting in the apartment alone. My mummy and daddy weren't home. Someone came through the door, but it was someone I hadn't seen before. He took me away. All I could do was cry; would I be safe or would I die? I wanted my mummy and daddy.

Declan Pickavance (11)
St Bede's Catholic School & Sixth Form College, Lanchester

The Thing

I was amazed. It was unbelievable. 'Twas hilarious.
It's that funny, I can't tell you, even if I wanted to.
You wouldn't believe me. If I tell you, you can't tell
anyone. No, I won't tell you. No, it's too astonishing.
Still can't tell you, OK, it is nothing.

James McDonald (12)
St Bede's Catholic School & Sixth Form College, Lanchester

Morocco And Me

I was horse riding; there was a competition coming up. Amazingly, Hellen asked me to attend. My response? Yes.
Competition day came. I wasn't nervous. I was riding Morocco, jumping two metres, it was something to remember for life. Winning the trophy with my name engraved, going home a winner!

Lauren Jane Field (12)
St Bede's Catholic School & Sixth Form College, Lanchester

Rain

I shade under the little dryness of the old oak. I wrench my raincoat from my back and thrust it over my head. The droplets pour to the ground like tears from a sobbing child. I stumble as sparks of lightning strike across the gloomy sky. Where do I go?

Emily Cowan (12)
St Bede's Catholic School & Sixth Form College, Lanchester

The Scream

Bright glittering stars were light to my eyes as I walked along the dark, frightening path. I swear that I heard what seemed like a young girl's scream. I started walking faster until I felt safe. I felt glum and scared. I would never know the reason for that scream.

Phillipa Close (11)
St Bede's Catholic School & Sixth Form College, Lanchester

Fat Broke At Night

Mammoth black boots pound the floor. Beady eyes lock onto their target. The big man's hungry. The clock strikes midnight, others are asleep. Drunk on whisky, lumbering about the houses seeking his victim. A blood-red coat catches my eye. He turns and stares at me … 'What? Oh hello Santa.'

Robert Owens (12)
St Bede's Catholic School & Sixth Form College, Lanchester

African Quest

I was walking through the African plains. In front of
me was a swamp full of crocodiles. I jumped from
rock to rock but the rocks were hippopotamuses. I
leapt for the ledge where I got bitten by a poisonous
snake.

Would I live or would I die?

Eleanor Fenwick (12)
St Bede's Catholic School & Sixth Form College, Lanchester

Goal

Number 7 running up the wing, past one, past another. The goalie's up the field; screaming and shouting. With the ball gliding through the air like a frisbee, players await. As the ball continues to spin and crowd's becoming anxious, number 9 springs from ground, heading home the winning goal.

Sophie Coyle (14)
St Bede's Catholic School & Sixth Form College, Lanchester

World Cup Dreams

It's been a long and hard World Cup campaign.
Players enter the pitch - World Cup final. Intense
pressure. Young talented footballer desperate to
shine.
It's been a stretched match. Last minute; young
player receives ball, shoots, scores! Shuts eyes in joy.
Runs, smashes head off goalpost. Hospitalised. Dies.

Ian McKie (13)
St Bede's Catholic School & Sixth Form College, Lanchester

Horsey

We flew over the last fence, adrenaline rushing
through my body. We galloped fiercely towards the
finishing box. That's all I can remember …
Now here I lie on the floor in tremendous pain and in
glory no more.

Rebecca Wilson (13)
St Bede's Catholic School & Sixth Form College, Lanchester

A Twist In The Tale

One mouse. All alone. Contemplates its chances.
Quite high, they are. Run for it! Cat appears, too
far from home. Yellow eyes lock on target. Heart
pounding race. Split second stop. Labyrinth of
furniture. Turn around. Cat can't move. All tangled
up. A real twist in the tail!

Becky McDonald (14)
St Bede's Catholic School & Sixth Form College, Lanchester

Chessboard

Its appearance was like a chessboard. It glared down at me with its big green glassy eyes. Its teeth were enormous and pointy. They took the resemblance of a knife. The cage rattled furiously as the lock was removed. The lock dropped on the floor as the puppy ran out.

Toni Kearney (13)
St Bede's Catholic School & Sixth Form College, Lanchester

Freedom

Bindey the parrot flew wild and free. Her friend Leo was locked up and unhappy. Bindey did all she could to get him out but Leo's keeper pushed her about. Then one day she knocked his cage on the floor so when the door opened he was free once more.

Caitlin Thompson (12)
St Bede's Catholic School & Sixth Form College, Lanchester

Holiday Trip

We were on our way to Spain. When the plane started moving and shaking. The gas masks dropped. People were squealing like pigs. Suddenly I felt us drop, we were falling to our death. I was only five years old and even I knew we were all doomed to die.

Joe Grigg (12)
St Bede's Catholic School & Sixth Form College, Lanchester

The Howling

Suddenly it dawned on her - she was doomed. The girl stood back in horror as the monstrous jet-black hound snarled and growled, its coat soaked and dripping with blood. The beast's stomach growled hungrily. The dog took aim, leapt and … there was a fifteen-minute break at the cinema.

Erin Lee-Dodd (11)
St Bede's Catholic School & Sixth Form College, Lanchester

Twin Towers

It all started on September 11th 2001 - a day that nobody will ever forget. Two planes were hijacked and flown into the World Trade Center towers killing so many people in the towers and on the ground. No one on-board any of the hijacked aircraft survived the impact.

Kelly Cook (11)

St Bede's Catholic School & Sixth Form College, Lanchester

105

The Life Of A Mouse

Everything is so big. Everyone hates me. I need
food to live but it is like I live for food. I love food.
When people see me they scream when it is I who is
scared.
Last night a human gave me the cut. Life's not fair,
I'm dead now.

Matthew Renwick (13)
St Bede's Catholic School & Sixth Form College, Lanchester

In A Daze

I was walking along the street in a daydream when I thought about a helicopter flying through the air, then crashing into a lamp post …

When I came out of my daze I realised I had actually walked into the lamp post and was sitting on the floor, confused.

Jiff Carr (13)

St Bede's Catholic School & Sixth Form College, Lanchester

Wonderful Life

I've often heard people say that life is a wonderful gift
but is life really wonderful when you're being bullied
or have no friends? When you hear of murders and
fights? Always watching your back, scared, anxious.
If life is such a gift why is it abused?

Douglas Patterson (13)
St Bede's Catholic School & Sixth Form College, Lanchester

Untitled

The screeching burned my eyes as they came to a stop. They looked like the gates to my house but were brighter. I walked through them and stopped. There was a bright light in front of me. Someone shouted, 'Don't walk into the light.' And then it came to me ...

Christopher Whitton-Hart (13)

St Bede's Catholic School & Sixth Form College, Lanchester

In My Dream

I was in the battlefield with my rifle, pulling from enemy lines. I got back to base and called it a day. 'Twas next morning. Went back into battle against the enemy - shooting away, killing soldiers. I reloaded, thinking I should wake up. It was hard. What's happened?

Michael Maughan (13)
St Bede's Catholic School & Sixth Form College, Lanchester

Slingshot

My heart's beating like a drum. The springs are tightening and the pod is going lower. The big rubber bands are tensing, as I am closing my eyes while the countdown goes from 9 to 1.
9, 8, 7, 6, 5, 4, 3, 2, 1, *bang!* - The slingshot!

Sam Rooney (12)
St Bede's Catholic School & Sixth Form College, Lanchester

The Mystery

They ran as fast as they could when they heard the scream. As they got there it was already too late. The girl was dead! Nothing they could do. One of the boys rang the police on his mobile. By the time they got there it was too late.

Nick Andrews (12)
St Bede's Catholic School & Sixth Form College, Lanchester

112

The Shadow

The door opened and a shadow, dripping wet, came in the room. He lifted up a rope, after that I blacked out … Wow I'm dead!
I woke up in a place I had never been. It was white and bright. Oh no, I was dead.

Daniel Monaghan (12)
St Bede's Catholic School & Sixth Form College, Lanchester

113

The Roller Coaster

I got on the roller coaster and it left the station. We went up a steep hill. We went very fast then we came to some sharp turns. I was thrown about wildly while my seat belt snapped and I fell off fast into the fog. I was, sadly, dead.

Peter Nixon (12)
St Bede's Catholic School & Sixth Form College, Lanchester

The Mysterious Building

We were giggling and chatting on our way from the car. There was deadly silence around us and there was a massive building in front of us. We climbed the stairs wondering what was happening. We were surrounded by the noise of roars … Newcastle had just scored a goal.

Callum Rogan (14)
St Bede's Catholic School & Sixth Form College, Lanchester

I Was Or I Wasn't A Hero

I was a superhero. On the night of 21st December
I was catching thieves and bullies. Every night I had
to search for them. When my mission ended I was
jumping straight onto buildings.
Suddenly I tripped and when I fell down … I was on
my bed. Wake up!

Jim Vofteras (11)
St Bede's Catholic School & Sixth Form College, Lanchester

The Fall Of Terror

There I was, falling backwards with knots in my stomach, crying, wondering whether I was going to live or die. So I closed my eyes and counted to twenty. The moment of truth. I opened my eyes, at the same time screaming.
Finally the plane was up in the air.

Rebecca Turner (12)
St Bede's Catholic School & Sixth Form College, Lanchester

117

Madeleine

Poor little girl left alone; no one to defend her when someone who isn't a parent comes home. Fear and wonder for finding her. Non-stop searching for her around the world … will she be missing forever? Or soon, will we see her running for her mum?

Jessica Coyle (12)
St Bede's Catholic School & Sixth Form College, Lanchester

The Towers

I looked out of my window and saw the most terrifying scene. Planes flying into both of the towers, one after the other. Smoke and flames covering like a thick grey blanket. People jumping from the building to escape the horrors, or dying in flames. September 11th - a terrible day.

Lucy Redshaw (12)
St Bede's Catholic School & Sixth Form College, Lanchester

Alone

I am lying asleep with my brothers and sisters then I wake up … don't know where I am? Strange place, strange people. My parents are out searching, they can't find me. People everywhere waiting and watching out for me. I'm all alone, no one there to listen to my cry.

Hollie Hicks (12)
St Bede's Catholic School & Sixth Form College, Lanchester

Bullies

One day I was walking down the street minding my own business and some lads pushed me to the floor. I tried getting up but he kicked me in the face. Then they all started, I got put in hospital for a week, just because I was ginger!

Michael Atkinson (12)
St Bede's Catholic School & Sixth Form College, Lanchester

The Terrifying Day

One day the most terrible thing happened. I was walking back from school when I saw a mysterious figure. I looked around to see what was happening when suddenly someone grabbed my mouth. I started to panic. My friend came and quickly phoned the police. The person ran off.

Carly Taylor (12)
St Bede's Catholic School & Sixth Form College, Lanchester

Behind You!

One day it was really sunny. Me and my friends were playing lots of different games like 'levo'. When it got dark we started playing 'dead letter'. Everyone was hiding from the opposite team. I was by myself, hiding, when I heard something behind me … 'Boo!' It was Carly Taylor.

Roisin Smith (12)
St Bede's Catholic School & Sixth Form College, Lanchester

Only Dreaming

I have loads of things running through my mind from promises to memories, friends and enemies. But from all of that I have none … I get bullied. As I toss and turn in bed, holding my teddy to my heart, I then think of what's been happening. Actually, I'm dreaming.

Rebecca McAloan (12)
St Bede's Catholic School & Sixth Form College, Lanchester

My Imagination Made Me Hear Things

I was walking along an alleyway. When I stopped, so did they. When I got home I took off my coat. It brushed against the wall. I heard footsteps again. My imagination had fooled me. I thought the buttons on my sleeve were footsteps. *Silly me,* I thought, *never mind.*

Catherine Burnham-King (12)
St Bede's Catholic School & Sixth Form College, Lanchester

Dark Night

It was dark. All the lights had gone off. I rushed through the street. I heard a strange sound behind me. I turned round but I still wasn't sure. There was no one to be seen. I could hear voices getting louder. What could it be … ? I was dreaming!

Simone Burn (13)
St Bede's Catholic School & Sixth Form College, Lanchester

The Killer

The sun was beaming. Sweat was dripping from my brow.
'Group C4 to the killer,' was bellowed.
I had butterflies. I moved forward to the killer. I clambered into the small hole. I thought it was the end. Then I slid down the huge slide at Mr Twisters.

Jordan Jewitt (14)
St Bede's Catholic School & Sixth Form College, Lanchester

The Girl

Not considering her feelings, I laughed at how she was. I knew one day the tables would turn. It would be me who would lose it all, me who would trip and fall. I knew she was plastic, willing to break at any time. All she knew … so was I.

Autumn Craggs (14)
St Bede's Catholic School & Sixth Form College, Lanchester

The Big Day

It was the big day of the final. I got up, got ready, looked around, where was my cue? I couldn't find it anywhere, but then I saw my dog chewing something. I looked in shock - my dog was chewing on my cue! I then cried for days on end.

Jonny Bradley (14)
St Bede's Catholic School & Sixth Form College, Lanchester

The Man

The young girl was creeping through the darkness. Her heart was thumping fast and hard. She didn't know where he was. *He could be anywhere,* she thought, *anywhere at all.* She looked in the cupboards and under the bed. He wasn't there. She didn't know he didn't exist.

William Connolly (14)
St Bede's Catholic School & Sixth Form College, Lanchester

Why Me?

The second half of a cricket match, Cook is in bat with Warne bowling. He bowls … *crack!* Cook has been hit on the leg with the ball. He falls to the ground; he has broken his leg. They need someone to play. They pick me from the crowd. Me, why?

Hannah Foy (14)
St Bede's Catholic School & Sixth Form College, Lanchester

131

Snow Day

Out of my window I saw nothing but snow. The
snow must have been three feet deep. The radio said
all schools closed. I was so happy. I could not wait
to go out with my friends … but the door wouldn't
open so I was stuck cleaning all day.

Joseph Morton (14)
St Bede's Catholic School & Sixth Form College, Lanchester

That Day

It is the big day. I've been ready for months but not today, the one day I'm not so ready for it. Oh, what can I do? Butterflies taking over, nervous, afraid, ready. Why did I say I'd do this stupid task? OK here goes - 3, 2, 1, game on.

Patrick Lee (14)
St Bede's Catholic School & Sixth Form College, Lanchester

The Classroom

Bang! I heard a noise. I saw a woman standing there crying. *Bang!* I heard it again. I looked at her. *Bang!* But she said nothing then suddenly said, 'Get up!' I immediately arose in my classroom with my teacher slamming her hand off of my desk.

Andrew Swan (14)

St Bede's Catholic School & Sixth Form College, Lanchester

Golden Beach

This is the most exciting moment ever, getting faster and faster, no way am I going to stop too soon. The moon shines down on us. It feels like I'm running away from someone. The sea is so calm. The sand is so soft. I'm galloping alone on the beach.

Remy Moor (12)
St Bede's Catholic School & Sixth Form College, Lanchester

The Window

Out the window watching the birds fly, the grass
swishes, the trees crinkle as the leaves drop. The
fields are full of sheep, little lambs, rabbits jumping
happily across the field but then the rain comes. The
animals hide, the thunder clashes, the dullness of the
sky reigns here.

Ryan Brown (12)
St Bede's Catholic School & Sixth Form College, Lanchester

Speed

Sitting, waiting. Slowly the fast machine starts.
Halfway up the tunnel it suddenly shoots up in speed.
It loops, dives and goes upside down. I knew I would
be sick just looking at the magnificent beast. It was
the top speed - 63mph. It was over - The Hulk.

Jack Teichman (12)
St Bede's Catholic School & Sixth Form College, Lanchester

Football Factory

The two teams of warriors hold their heads up high as they march onto the battlefield. Fear trembles in the hearts of the soldiers as the head boys head to the centre circle. They make eye contact as they firmly shake hands. The whistle blows and all hell breaks loose.

Kieran Martin (12)
St Bede's Catholic School & Sixth Form College, Lanchester

Our New Teacher

I sat there waiting for our new teacher to arrive.
Everybody sitting talking. That was about to change.
I thought it was ridiculous. Anyone but her. Everyone
would tease me and my reputation would go
downhill, and then … as the door opened, Katie said,
'Look Lauren, it's your mum!'

Lauren Wilkinson (12)
St Bede's Catholic School & Sixth Form College, Lanchester

Always Left On Christmas Day

My ears ache from the screeching of my younger
sisters. I turn over feeling extremely cold and still
tremendously tired. As I slowly open my swollen,
matted eyes, there's paper, wrapping paper. I glance
down towards the floor realising I must get ready.
They always leave me on Christmas Day.

Becky Brown (14)
St Bede's Catholic School & Sixth Form College, Lanchester

Crazy Nabraska

'Come on Drew, keep rowing, they're gaining on us.'
We were in the outskirts of Nabraska being chased
by giant man-eating moles.
'Argh!' Drew fell out. I make a left turn. Sugar canes!
Waterfall ahead, must jump out unscathed, only small
amount of health.
Damn you level 17.

Dominic Hewitson (14)
St Bede's Catholic School & Sixth Form College, Lanchester

141

The Walk Of Terror

Walking down the corridor … a total nightmare.
Pupils shouting and screaming my name, saying
inappropriate words. I try running but people just
trip me up. I should just turn around, but I can't, I'm
already halfway down the hallway. Someone pulls me
into a corner, everyone crowds around.

Nicola Brown (14)
St Bede's Catholic School & Sixth Form College, Lanchester

Big Bang

Bang! It awoke, gabbling and screaming. It came towards me, mouth open ready to get me, eyes shut tightly, hitting me with its poison, its giant footsteps quivering around me, pulling me side to side. It hit me. My baby sister wanted a cuddle from her big loving sister.

Stacie Darroch (13)
St Bede's Catholic School & Sixth Form College, Lanchester

Alone In The Dark

Alone in the dark. All the lights are out. Shadows surround me but I'm all by myself. The lights come on. Everyone shouts, 'Surprise!' I scream with shock. Lots of people in my house. I am surprised - it's my birthday party and everyone's there. I cry, I am so happy.

Kimberley Lauder (13)
St Bede's Catholic School & Sixth Form College, Lanchester

144

Racing Days

Speeding round the hairpin bend, the g-force was unbearable. I was leading the race, so close to the championship. Down into fifth gear, round the last bend … the door flew open. The manager of the store angrily told me to get out of the car. I'm too young to drive.

Hayley Arckless (13)
St Bede's Catholic School & Sixth Form College, Lanchester

The New Kid

At school a new kid was standing in the middle of the playground with a cake. Five boys called Jason, Freddy, Shane, Sean and Gary made friends with him and played with him. But everything they played was bad luck so they said, 'Go away.' Their luck was back.

Shane Connolfy (12)
St Bede's Catholic School & Sixth Form College, Lanchester

The Final Face Off (Morgan Vs Cheong)

Morgan has just head-butted Cheong. Look at the blood spurting from the top of his Flash Gordon mask in today's arm wrestling championship. Timeout, ow that's dirty from Cheong, spitting in Morgan's face. But what's this … yes! Cheong's arm has snapped and we now have a new arm wrestling champion - Morgan the Destroyer.

Lee Clark (12)

St Bede's Catholic School & Sixth Form College, Lanchester

The Evil Jessica

She ran faster, faster than her legs could carry her. She was running away form her sister. She fell. Jessica had her now. Suddenly her friend jumped in and hit Jessica. Jessica started crying, 'You hurt my finger.' Then she got a plastic table and hit her over the head.

Danielle Stafford (12)
St Bede's Catholic School & Sixth Form College, Lanchester

Clumsy

I stumble down the street, knocking down plant
pots, running into walls all the time. I'm clumsy as a
playful badger. Everybody thinks I'm drunk. I walk
into a bar, *clunk!* I'm not drunk, I'm just clumsy.
Well, I have just been shot!

Max Simpson (12)
St Bede's Catholic School & Sixth Form College, Lanchester

Hero

I jumped out of my hut. I was getting shot but I ran and shot all of my opponents. I reloaded my gun and got ready for the second go. I had them in my sight, they didn't stand a chance. Just then my mam called me in for tea.

Isidore Lapsatis (11)
St Bede's Catholic School & Sixth Form College, Lanchester

The Three Men At War

Connor, Ryan and I were dropped at the front line. Ryan was taking out loads then got shot in the leg. Connor was a first aider. I called him. He got into the hotel where Ryan was. He patched Ryan up. The building was surrounded by mines. Help us!

Lee Armstrong (12)
St Bede's Catholic School & Sixth Form College, Lanchester

151

The Day I Bashed Into A Lamp Post

I was running - they were chasing me. They kept shouting things at me but I ignored them. What's the rush? *Don't turn round,* I thought, *keep running faster and faster.* I did. The next thing I knew I was on the floor. I had bashed into a lamp post.

Rozfynne Barron (12)
St Bede's Catholic School & Sixth Form College, Lanchester

Untitled

I can't wait to be 18 so I can drink alcohol, smoke, gamble, drive, get married and have kids. But once you take a moment to realise that this can turn tragic - gamble your house, get cancer, crash your car, with kids pulling out your hair … I wanna stay young!

Liam Marshall (12)
St Bede's Catholic School & Sixth Form College, Lanchester

153

The Flaming Building

One night I was lying in bed when all of a sudden I was awoken by screams. I sat up to see flames outside my window. Panicking I jumped out of bed to get my mum and dad. I explained and the fire brigade came.

Jordan Mavin (12)
St Bede's Catholic School & Sixth Form College, Lanchester

Untitled

I woke up, went to the mirror, big red lumps staring at me, 'Eugh!' I cried. 'What are those terrible things on my face?' I was dreading going to school - people would laugh at me and stare too. It started itching. I itched. It got worse. Chickenpox - nooo!

Emma Shaw (12)
St Bede's Catholic School & Sixth Form College, Lanchester

The Corridor

I raced along the corridor. I heard people screaming.
I was sure there was someone following me. I
couldn't find the door, the door that would lead me
to safety. Had I passed it? No, there it was, just a few
metres away. I had made it to my detention.

Anne-Louise Oates (14)
St Bede's Catholic School & Sixth Form College, Lanchester

The Glow

One gloomy night the ground is freezing. I hear a shriek and now I'm scared. Drip. I spin round to acknowledge that it's just a rusty drainpipe. I stagger forwards down an alley to see a glimmering glow. I approach it with fear and excitement, step by step … it disappears.

David Gornall (14)
St Bede's Catholic School & Sixth Form College, Lanchester

The Punch

Lying on the cold wet floor, unaware of my surroundings. I think I'm dead but this doesn't seem like Heaven, or what I thought it would be anyway. Wait! I hear people, sirens. I think I'm in hospital. I remember having a fight. I was knocked unconscious ... oh no!

Emma Maſpass (13)
St Bede's Catholic School & Sixth Form College, Lanchester

The Wolf

I entered Alaska, I was going to try dog sleighing. I decided I wanted to go trekking. I wanted to go in the forest. Then I heard something weird. It was a scary noise. I started to run home frightened. A wolf howling in the wind, echoing through my mind.

Emma Dixon (14)
St Bede's RC Comprehensive School, Peterlee

Cliffhanger (The Ride)

Butterflies in my stomach, hands shaking, my heart beating as fast as a racing car. My hands squeezing very tightly on the bars, my ears going to burst with all the screaming and shouting. As the voices counting down music get louder - *whoosh!* The fast cliffhanger shot up.

Jade Naylor
St Bede's RC Comprehensive School, Peterlee

Rover

Pulling ropes tightly wrapped around my wrists,
dragging me across the floor. Blood was pouring
down my knees. Noises filled my ears, ropes getting
tighter as I get further on. I grapple with the enemy
… I quickly grab a hold of his soft small neck.
Another dog walk gone wrong!

Melissa Wood (14)
St Bede's RC Comprehensive School, Peterlee

Survival

My feet crawl over rubble, my hands holding onto cracked walls, screams and blood cover the smoky air filling my fast-pumping lungs. My heart is beating like a machine as flashes of red and blue lights cove the surroundings. I've managed to set myself free from the Twin Towers.

Sarah Little (14)
St Bede's RC Comprehensive School, Peterlee

Don't Wake It!

I creep away as quietly as possible hoping not to wake 'it', for 'it' will make a giant roar. I get so far away, I'm so close, but then suddenly I make a loud crashing noise. No, I've set 'it' away, now the baby's going to be up all night!

Stacey Haff (14)
St Bede's RC Comprehensive School, Peterlee

Falling

I felt myself falling. I didn't know where I was,
terrified at the thought of where I was gonna go
next. I could feel air rushing past me. I saw a light at
the bottom. It was getting closer, very near now, I
was there now, I … woke up!

David Hughes (13)
St Bede's RC Comprehensive School, Peterlee

A Deep Darkness

I squinted as a blinding light entered the room and a dark figure emerged from behind the door. I heard the footsteps as the figure walked towards me. I closed my eyes, hoping the darkness would envelop me again. I felt a cold hand shaking me … I hate waking up!

Ross Bridges (14)
St Bede's RC Comprehensive School, Peterlee

Never Late Again

I can just remember sticking my hand out into the road, waiting for a taxi because my bus had gone, that was the third time in one week! Now I don't have to worry about that anymore because … no, I haven't been sacked, but I do have a Gucci watch!

Kirsty McAndrew (14)
St Bede's RC Comprehensive School, Peterlee

Couldn't See

I'd woken up from the operation. I could barely see a thing. I wasn't hungry at all. The toast I had tasted horrible. It was burnt. After, I tried to eat the burnt toast. Believe it or not the only person I wanted to see was my brother. My bro.

Ciara Welsh (12)
St Bede's RC Comprehensive School, Peterlee

Perfect Feeling

It's nearly my turn, so scared, what if it goes wrong
or I'm out of tune? X-Factor judges will be sitting
there staring at me. Hannah's going to press play
soon. What if I start too late? Steph and Hannah will
do it perfect. Now the song: What A Feeling!

Lauren Dawson (11)
St Bede's RC Comprehensive School, Peterlee

Bang!

It was so smooth and it was loaded. It was so shiny and cold. I thought about my ex-girlfriend and all the good times. I started crying and I had to do it. I was so miserable so I moved it close to my head and I gripped on.

Bang!

Adam Richardson (14)

St Bede's RC Comprehensive School, Peterlee

The Finale

The lights went off and the volume blasted out. The excitement rushed through me as I finally found out the finale. What's going to happen? Only time would tell. Then suddenly a noise, the fire drill. Yet the tension was too great so I stayed and sizzled in the cinema.

Rebecca Morton (14)
St Bede's RC Comprehensive School, Peterlee

Him

The decision was unbearable. He clenched the pink bottle as his hands sweat with anticipation. Screwing the lid off ever so slowly, he slid the brush as it sucked and squelched the liquid inside. His dry lips were refreshed as he delicately placed his lipgloss on. *Gorgeous*, he thought, smiling.

Emma Milburn (13)
St Bede's RC Comprehensive School, Peterlee

Next!

There it was, the word I dreaded … 'next'. I walked in and sat down. The light shone down on me. *What can I do? How can I escape?* I thought! I opened my mouth then fainted.

When I awoke, I felt a throbbing pain. I absolutely hate dentist appointments. *Ouch!*

Hannah Fahey (13)
St Bede's RC Comprehensive School, Peterlee

My Dream Man

My heart fluttered. My stomach turned. Why me?
The eye contact was ecstatic as he held me close in
his arms, his muscles rippling in the hot summer sun.
Bright colours in the sky as the sun set behind the
sea. Just about to kiss ... and I wake up. Damn!

Kristy Gorse (14)
St Bede's RC Comprehensive School, Peterlee

Sitting By The Sea

She sat by the sea collecting shells, the ocean
was delicately flowing over the sand. The seagulls
squawked and chatted to themselves. She felt the
soft sand between her toes, it was soft as cotton.
The sun was glistening down on the water as the sun
set, on her.

Beth Rawling (12)
St Bede's RC Comprehensive School, Peterlee

174

Crime Or Not?

I walked out of the shop. Alarms started screaming. I
ran. Police sprinted behind me. What had I done?
'Stop!'
Terrified, I hopped the wall in front of me. To my
surprise, a security guard was on the other side.
'You're nicked!'
'For taking a free sample of juice?'

Hayley Clarke (13)
St Bede's RC Comprehensive School, Peterlee

Space

It was dark, getting darker. The only light source was the stars. I've been falling for what seems an eternity, into a dark abyss. Oxygen running low, desperately needing help. A shuttle shoots by. I pray that they'll save me. The shuttle turns, hovers above me … I'm saved.

Richard Dring (12)
St Bede's RC Comprehensive School, Peterlee

My Fear

And there he was, lying on the bed, slowly being cut
open, blood going all over. I was staring at him; I felt
sorry for him. Scissors, knives, hands going into him.
And then he woke up, vet's telling me to allow him
to rest.
Me and Max walked home.

Leanne Movat (13)
St Bede's RC Comprehensive School, Peterlee

Race

We were up against the nastiest racing cars ever.
Razor-sharp chrome gleaming in the dark, weapons
shaking under roaring hoods. I shouted, 'Lose the
suckers!' Left, right, down the straight. Gunfire. Land
mine. *Boom!* One down with a menace on our tail.
Swish, spin, shift and fire ... *winner!*

Alan Richardson (13)
St Bede's RC Comprehensive School, Peterlee

Sleepy Waters

Shaking violently, gas masks dropped down. Heart thumping, I clipped on my seat belt. As the plane got nearer to the sea I sank in my seat. *Splash!* We plunged into the water. Gasping, my eyes opened. Shampoo? Conditioner? What the … ? Dozed off in the bath again. Silly old me!

Rebecca Evans (13)
St Bede's RC Comprehensive School, Peterlee

179

Auditions

Five, six, seven, eight, we were counted in. We smiled and flaunted our talent. Hops, kicks, spins and twirls. We faked our cheesy smiles. The audience clapping to the beat, singing along. I'm skipping about, others too. Clapping all around. Then we get praise. We are through to the X-Factor!

Ashley Bowdser (12)
St Bede's RC Comprehensive School, Peterlee

The Sound

The most terrifying noise. What was it? I grabbed a bat, my heart racing. I had to find it. Did I want to do this? Another screeching sound. I placed my hand on the door - I flung it open with all my might. To my amazement ... the cat was hungry.

Laura Nichols (14)
St Bede's RC Comprehensive School, Peterlee

Untitled

It was dark. My stomach ached. I reached out, my fingertips just touched it. I had to have it. It smelt brilliant but I had to jump over the dog that was protecting it. I took a huge leap and grabbed it. I swallowed huge chunks. Leftover dessert - yum!

Stephanie Armstrong (12)
St Bede's RC Comprehensive School, Peterlee

Do Or Die

I had to open it. It was do or die. I started to twist
… *smash!* I couldn't do it. I pushed down the lever.
It didn't go down. Why didn't it? I couldn't think why,
but finally the lever went down and it opened … I
had my beans on toast!

Lee Bowdfer (14)
St Bede's RC Comprehensive School, Peterlee

183

Untitled

My heart beating faster and faster as it was almost in my mouth. Trying to scream but nothing seemed to come out. Sweat began to stream down my face. The doors slammed shut. It approached. My hands stuck to the wall, my hearing blanked, my vision blurred. Was I dead?

Tia Laidlaw (13)
St Bede's RC Comprehensive School, Peterlee

Race On, Dreamer!

The breeze passing rapidly, sounds of galloping hooves, my heart beating faster, screaming crowds. The last furlong, panting Dreamer as flying hooves race head to head. Nearly there, no one ahead. The biggest race of the calendar! I could feel her tendons going upon the grass. Slowly ... we both disappeared.

Anna Pittam (13)
St Bede's RC Comprehensive School, Peterlee

Untitled

I stood on the rocky edge, looking over nervously. My heart started to race. My legs began to shake. I couldn't breathe. I started to tumble, bouncing from side to side. My whole life flashed before my eyes as I thought that the old, frayed, rough rope might suddenly snap!

Nicola Hutchinson (13)
St Bede's RC Comprehensive School, Peterlee

Untitled

I was in the cold and it was a dark, dusky night and nobody was about, but out the corner of my eye I saw something move in the bushes. I was scared, petrified. Nothing was coming out. It stopped moving but there it was. It popped out and pounced.

Jonathan Ward (13)
St Bede's RC Comprehensive School, Peterlee

187

I Heard A Noise

My heart thumped louder as I gently opened the door to the dark room! I raised my weak fingers and reached for the light switch. After a few blinking flashes, the light came on. As I took one more small step, I saw a white, ghostly shadow standing before me!

Sarah Young (13)
St Bede's RC Comprehensive School, Peterlee

The White Wolf

I stopped. They surrounded me, their eyes gleaming in the moonlight, baring their teeth, growling, snarling. Suddenly, an icy wind blew around, then a snow-white wolf appeared. She walked gracefully in front of me. *Bang!* I was knocked to the ground. She sniffed me. I realised she accepted me!

Amy-Louise Wood (12)
St Bede's RC Comprehensive School, Peterlee

Beano At The Beach

The bright sun and blue sea glistened in my eyes.
I prepared to go for a gallop on my horse, Beano.
There were butterflies in my grumbling tummy
and Beano was getting wound up like a clockwork
toy. No longer did I know, I was off into the sunny
horizon.

Lucy Kemp (12)
St Bede's RC Comprehensive School, Peterlee

The Crash

I feel the wind gush past me as I ride in the back of my dad's car. Faster and faster we go until suddenly, we crash. I see the car all broken and smashed, but where is my dad? Where has he gone? Is he gone forever? Oh … not now!

Rebecca Lambe (12)
St Bede's RC Comprehensive School, Peterlee

191

Car Crash

Me and my dog were walking round the corner of a house. That's when my dog saw a cat. 'Jack!' I screamed. He didn't listen. He's too strong. That's when I fell. I yelped. I got dragged onto the main road. A car came. I closed my eyes and screamed.

Laura Bowes (11)
St Bede's RC Comprehensive School, Peterlee

Untitled

In my life I enjoy singing because I am good at it, but when I get on stage I panic and I freeze. Nothing comes out and when it does, it doesn't sound right. But most of all I shake and I look at people's faces. I do nothing.

Rachael Steel (12)
St Bede's RC Comprehensive School, Peterlee

The Lonely Assassin

The stone-like eyes stared at me. I had turned my back. I looked down. My knees shook. I could feel my heartbeat. I turned to look at the strange-looking statue. It was gone. A shadow was forming. Tears ran down my face. Could this be the end of me?

Liam Irwin (12)
St Bede's RC Comprehensive School, Peterlee

Black Hole

One sunny day I went to Wet and Wild, it was great fun. I went on the Black Hole. It was light at first, then gradually got dark as night. I was in the water, drowning. I was whooshing side to side. I was afraid, then *splash!* I was out.

Paige Wilkinson (12)
St Bede's RC Comprehensive School, Peterlee

My Little Star

There's a star in the sky shining on through. The way it shines reminds me of you, how you stood out smiling so bright, but now you watch over me in the dark night. No matter where you may be or how far, you will always be my little star.

Gemma Turner (13)
St Bede's RC Comprehensive School, Peterlee

196

The Great Race

I feel sick; my stomach's churning … oops, and they're off! I scream, I shout. I don't feel too great but I see them. Running faster and faster they keep going. Think of the glory he could have. My baby is running … fingers crossed. My horse has won, *yes! Ha ha!*

Lauren Beff (14)
St Bede's RC Comprehensive School, Peterlee

197

Weird, Wonderful, Magical Tale

In the land of Todd where the dragons and leprechauns live, there is a beast that is evil and jolly. He eats little boys and girls but then gives pearls to the people of the world. No mercy from this beast - he will eat you as his bountiful, delicious feast.

Jacob Beeston (13)
St Bede's RC Comprehensive School, Peterlee

198

His Dream Come True

He sits alone in a café where no one goes, waiting for the woman of his dreams. Sitting 6am to 6pm, hoping she will see him. He sees her sitting on a park bench, blood rushing through his veins and his heart going too …
She asks him on a date!

Georgina Jessop (13)

St Bede's RC Comprehensive School, Peterlee

Different Sounds

A storm came louder and louder. People shouting.
Loud music with guitars and drums. People dancing
with suits, being watched by statues around.
Everyone being questioned. The sound was getting
quieter and quieter, then nothing …
My mam turned the television off! She was not
pleased at all. 'Bed, now!'

Laura Hemsley (13)
St Bede's RC Comprehensive School, Peterlee

200

The Ancient Classroom

The old, rickety classroom reeked and creaked. The windows were smashed, the rotten tables smelt of oil. The rusty hinges squeaked on the rotten wooden doors. The chairs that once looked shiny and clean, now they were splintered. The broken floorboards were damp … so what happened to the ancient classroom?

Katie Lincoln (14)
St Bede's RC Comprehensive School, Peterlee

201

Razor Blades And Blood

She reminisced on with videos and photos of her brother with her. She missed him so much, nothing was the same. Her reputation had gone the day of his death. She cried and sat inside the bath, razor in one hand, blood pouring down other, eyes shut … she's now gone!

Rebecca Murphy (13)
St Bede's RC Comprehensive School, Peterlee

Next

Here it is, the world I hate … *next*. So I got up, walked and sat on a stool, the lights shining in my eyes. I opened my mouth and fainted. I came round and I had a throbbing pain in my mouth … I hate dentist appointments!

Emma Maffen (13)
St Bede's RC Comprehensive School, Peterlee

203

The Night I Thought I'd Died

It was pitch-black. Noises echoed in the darkness. *What's that?* I thought. Someone was coming, their footsteps got louder, getting closer. A figure dressed in black stepped out of the darkness into the light caused by the lamp. He was masked. He had a gun ... *bang!* I woke up.

Alex Ward (13)
St Bede's RC Comprehensive School, Peterlee

The Drunken` Recruit

Cold, damp and sleeping in a muddy trench. I hate
war, the bloody mess of bodies and rifle shells is a
horrible sight. Gripping my rifle tight, friends all dead.
A mess of a life. But I wonder, *if I hadn't got drunk
that night, I wouldn't have signed up!*

Liam Hunt (12)
St Bede's RC Comprehensive School, Peterlee

205

Little Angels

She'd never seen the world. She was 9. What possessed her to walk away from the happiness? Only God knows. Friends saw the fear in her eyes as she fell over the edge. We all know she's happy now, away from the abuse, in Heaven with all the little angels.

Eden Graves (13)
St Bede's RC Comprehensive School, Peterlee

Ghost

I walked through the meadow, picking a flower as I stepped. I looked up and that's when I saw her running away ... so I followed.
Then I saw her lying dead on the grass, she was drenched in blood. I lay my flowers on her and walked away.

Hayley Honnor (13)
St Bede's RC Comprehensive School, Peterlee

The Big One

There I was, faced with him again. Big boy, bad boy.
The last time I woke up in hospital two weeks later.
He started throwing punches. I dodged a few then he
got me. It was my turn. I punched him in the nose.
The ref shouted, 'Knockout!'

Jordan Warren (12)
St Bede's RC Comprehensive School, Peterlee

Lost In The Forest

Standing in the middle of a forest my heart was pounding as a huge fierce lion was coming towards me … *crash!* Blood was pouring out of my arm. I had been bitten by a lion.

Catherine Downs (13)
St Bede's RC Comprehensive School, Peterlee

The Dark Woods

I was walking through the woods and I saw a big spaceship, then an alien came out. It was bong-eyed. It came over to me and said, 'Hello, I come in peace.' Its breath stank. He went to grab me. I ran home to tell my mummy.

Ryan Watson (13)
St Bede's RC Comprehensive School, Peterlee

Christmas Tree

I woke up and opened the door of my room. I started to tiptoe down the stairs to see my mum. She said, 'Close your eyes?'
I closed them. She opened the door ever so slightly. I opened my eyes. There they were. My presents … under the sparkling tree.

Jasmin Reed (12)
St Bede's RC Comprehensive School, Peterlee

The Race

I pulled away. I was dazed by the sun. I was being chased. Could I make it now? Could I get away? The sound of footsteps behind me. I had to speed up. It could be the end for me. No, not now. Keep on running. I've won the race.

Connor Beddow (13)
St Bede's RC Comprehensive School, Peterlee

Life-Threatening Dream

My body squeezed tight, I tried to wriggle my way out. The big object holding me gave up and, like a worm, I fell flat onto my face. Now's my chance, still trying to find my way out. He dunked me in the pot. I awoke … it's just a dream.

Ashleigh Purcell (14)

St Bede's RC Comprehensive School, Peterlee

The Race

The icy cold wind blew into my face as I quickly spun onto wet, hard gravel. My hand started shaking as I started to turn. I went faster and faster as the screeching noise coming from behind filled my ears. I crossed the line. I'd won the go-kart race.

Jessica Armstrong (13)
St Bede's RC Comprehensive School, Peterlee

214

Gears Of War

My surroundings demolished, my comrades fallen, I go to the broken statue, pick up half a face. I swear to kill the enemy. I gather my weapons, strap my armour on. I turn around, locust hordes march towards me … Monochrome aliens, their faces concealed, I crouch, aim and take fire!

Jonathan Chapman (14)
St Bede's RC Comprehensive School, Peterlee

215

Lightning

The electricity burst through my veins, my nerves
went haywire. My heart skipped beats. My body
jumped in the air, the metal dropped from my hand.
Cuts and bruises. Glue-like stuff had hardened in my
hair making it stand on end.
The lightning had stopped and I was alive.

Megan Bottomfey (14)
St Bede's RC Comprehensive School, Peterlee

On The Edge Of My Seat

I was lost, alone and had nowhere to go. I was scared but nobody could hear my screams. I could see movement in the distance but they couldn't see me. I felt hurt inside but unaware of what was yet to come.
And then it finished … the film was over.

Kevin Ghassemi (14)
St Bede's RC Comprehensive School, Peterlee

217

Don't Stop

I was running and running and running and I fell, I got back up as soon as I could and carried on running as fast as I could so I wasn't caught. I was running out of breath so I took one big breath but I got caught and tackled.

Alex Borthwick (14)
St Bede's RC Comprehensive School, Peterlee

Underwater

I take a deep breath. I'm in, in the water. Diving
down, I'm alone, surrounded by bubbly water.
Time seems to stop and all is calm. Suddenly I can't
breathe. I need air fast. I reach the surface, gasping.
Then a voice calls out, 'Have you finished that bath
yet?'

Catherine Hanson (14)
St Bede's RC Comprehensive School, Peterlee

Ahoy Mee Hearties

Drunken men singing while gliding across the open spread of white and blue nothingness. The captain calls out, 'Ahoy, ahoy.' His crewmates clink their bottles of rum in honour of their leader. A wave comes about to swallow the ship. *Crunch!* goes the ship. So long to the pirates.

Hannah Grainger (14)
St Bede's RC Comprehensive School, Peterlee

Wrong School, Wrong Clothes

As I walked through the school gates I noticed that people were staring at me, one teacher stopped his car, not to let me cross the road but because he wanted a good view of me. Then I suddenly noticed I was in the wrong school wearing pink clothes!

Andrew Moore (12)
St Bede's RC Comprehensive School, Peterlee

The Disaster

It was a disaster the day we went to the airport. We were there for hours, it was time for us to board. We got stopped at the gates, got sent home, couldn't go. They phoned us saying there was a flight from Nottingham on Wednesday so we went there.

Annie Bogie (13)
St Bede's RC Comprehensive School, Peterlee

222

Cracking Comedy

I had practised all summer, but when the night came my mind went blank. I was addressed on stage: Caitlan and her comedy by Head Teacher Joe. Fits of hysterics were followed by cheers. The atmosphere was amazing and I didn't want it to end. It was a fab experience.

Caitlan Quinney (13)
St Bede's RC Comprehensive School, Peterlee

My First Time

'You ready?' he asked.

'Yes,' I answered.

He started to tear into my skin, a spit of blood. I whimper, he asks if he should stop … I disagree. He starts again, tears roll down my face as he enters my body. He stops. I jump up and thank my dentist.

Yasmin Tomlinson (13)
St Bede's RC Comprehensive School, Peterlee

Scared

I entered. First came the splash of water. 'Not bad,'
I said to myself. Then came the snarling and growling
along with the sound of rattling cages. A loud roar
sounded and I ran away from the sounds, away from
the rattling cages.
'So, how was the zoo?' asked Mum.

Stacey Hogarth (13)
St Bede's RC Comprehensive School, Peterlee

225

The Scary Routine

It loomed up in front of me, a fortress of agony.
People go in there against their will to pay in money.
It almost drains away your energy and boredom sets
in. People push in metal carts so they can get more
items.
'No!'
That's right … yes, it is Asda.

Shannen Kelly (13)
St Bede's RC Comprehensive School, Peterlee

New Day

Waiting in the queue, butterflies in my stomach, gates opened, I sat in the seat, safety harness clicking as I pulled it down, blasting 200 feet on the cliff-hanger, gripping tight as my stomach lifted. Eyes closed tight, this is the end of a dream … A new day starts.

Shelby Graham (13)
St Bede's RC Comprehensive School, Peterlee

227

The Jump

I was going bungee jumping today. When I got there I started to feel sick. They started to strap me up. I was going up and up. I jumped … the cord snapped. My life flashed. I was gone - nothing but bright light … then I woke up … it was a dream.

Craig Drummond (13)
St Bede's RC Comprehensive School, Peterlee

The World War

On a Saturday night I was in the World War against a gang called the Vanguards. Suddenly monsters emerged from nowhere. They started killing everyone. I was wondering what was happening. Then one came behind me. It was like a werewolf biting a human. Then they charged … I woke up!

Kieron Wood (13)
St Bede's RC Comprehensive School, Peterlee

My African Life

I was walking through an African forest to explore.
I'd always wanted to go there. I saved up all my
money to go. It cost a million pounds. My African
friends left me alone. Suddenly two lions jumped on
me and ripped me apart ... I died a horrible death.

Jake Harrriman (13)
St Bede's RC Comprehensive School, Peterlee

All Alone

My hands shook. My spine shivered. Yes, I was worrying. The dark, ghostly room was haunting my dreams. I woke up, my hair was drenched with the sweat pouring rapidly out of me. I screamed at my sister, 'Wake up, wake up!' But she didn't and I was all alone.

Hannah Farneff (12)
St Bede's RC Comprehensive School, Peterlee

231

Untitled

Running to get away, messages screaming at me to stop, give in. I could hear them again and again. Then something grabbed me. I struggled. Its force was too tight. The pain became so bad I had to fall to the ground. My eyes closed, my pain ended. It's over!

Kimberley Howe (12)
St Bede's RC Comprehensive School, Peterlee

Untitled

My heart stomped. My breathing heavy, I stopped and looked behind. 'Phew,' no one there. Then I heard them. First slowly and then faster. Suddenly two tall dark figures appeared to make a run for it. But they were too fast, they grabbed me - I fell to the ground.

Becky Robinson (12)
St Bede's RC Comprehensive School, Peterlee

Just A Dream!

There we were … pushed to the edge. Literally!
We heard each other's hearts beating like a trotting
horse. It's scary to think we were held hostage
for such a long time. Suddenly the cliff rocked, it
crumbled! There we lay - dead!
Buzzzzz! Buzzzzz! My alarm! I must have been
dreaming!

Stephanie Beddeff (12)
St Bede's RC Comprehensive School, Peterlee

It's All A Dream

I was standing in my bedroom, it felt empty. My mind was spinning. I didn't know what to do until the windows started to flap. Things were moving all over. I really didn't know what was happening … then I fainted and woke up in the morning … It was a dream.

Lauren Anderson (12)
St Bede's RC Comprehensive School, Peterlee

A Day At The Dentist

Terrified, I was all by myself with no one to hold on to. Then the drill came closer and closer. I felt like screaming. I gripped hold of my top, squeezing it as hard as I could. I felt so scared.
Then the dentist said, 'Well done! You did great!'

Rebecca Graney (12)
St Bede's RC Comprehensive School, Peterlee

The Chase

The air blew in my face as I stuck my head out of the window to see the police hot on my tail. I looked up to see the police chopper with a spotlight on my stolen car. They rammed me into the wall, my legs crippled. It was over.

Sam Brahimi (14)
St Bede's RC Comprehensive School, Peterlee

Exciting Rush

The ground was rushing madly past me, everything
was a blur. My ears felt like they were going to
explode they were so compressed. My stomach was
churning more and more, I felt as if I was going to be
sick. This was the ride of my life, an aeroplane.

David Williams (14)
St Bede's RC Comprehensive School, Peterlee

Rush

I was in the car. We started to go faster. My dad tried to brake. The accelerator was stuck. We went faster, trees flashing beside as we approached a cliff. The car was going too fast to turn, we were going to die. The car rushed off the edge. *Splash!*

Adam Timney (13)
St Bede's RC Comprehensive School, Peterlee

239

The Simulator

I shot up into the air, passing the clouds as I flew into space, stars twinkling in the distance. Suddenly I saw a large rock appearing in front of me. Meteor shower! *Boom!*

'Mam, can I have another pound for that simulator ride please?'

Daniel Scott (14)
St Bede's RC Comprehensive School, Peterlee

World War II

As Liam ran down the street, bombs dropped down from the air, they hit everywhere, killing mothers and babies. When Liam approached the shelter another bomb was dropped. It hit the church, the church shattered and collapsed to the ground as World War II broke out.

Michael Ritson (13)
St Bede's RC Comprehensive School, Peterlee

Sad And Poor Boy To Happy Boy

It is my birthday. I don't get many presents because we're struggling money-wise. I get £5. I am so pleased. It will pay towards the electric bill. I am watching telly and then there is a sudden shake. Loads of presents appear and I don't know what happened …

James Anderson (14)
St Bede's RC Comprehensive School, Peterlee

242

Oblivion

Round and round, upside down, back to front.
I jump, I jerk, I twist, I turn. Heart racing, blood
pumping, jaw locked.
'Stacey, Stacey! You're hurting my hand.'
I'm falling faster and faster, closer and closer, round
and round, upside down, back to front. I jump, I jerk.
Oblivion!

Samantha Adamson (14)
St Bede's RC Comprehensive School, Peterlee

Big Day

She smiled in the mirror and twirled. She ran her hands down the soft silk. She walked out of the house and stepped into the shiny limousine. 'You look beautiful!' her mam said.
Eventually they arrived. The wedding bells rang as she opened the big, tall, wooden church door.

Lauren Robson (14)
St Bede's RC Comprehensive School, Peterlee

244

The Alley

Walking down a deserted alley on a pitch-black Hallowe'en night. Watching my iced white breath rising up to the full moon. A shadow rushed across the old narrow wall. Then a crash. Rooted to the spot. Suddenly there was a stampeding heartbeat. Then I saw it ... a hedgehog!

Jack Johnson (14)
St Bede's RC Comprehensive School, Peterlee

Untitled

She jumped up out of bed excitedly. Her alarm clock hadn't gone off! She panicked. She hadn't packed. She ran around so quickly that she ran out of breath. As she went to open the door she looked at the calendar … she wasn't going on holiday until tomorrow!

Hannah Pickering (14)
St Bede's RC Comprehensive School, Peterlee

The Dark Night

As I lay in bed my old rags offered a bit of warmth to my body. The shadow of the old oak tree waved in my face. A creak sounded through the silence of the night, the sound was of my mum's wardrobe where my grandad's medals were … Silence.

Adam Stokoe (13)
St Bede's RC Comprehensive School, Peterlee

247

Fire!

During the bitter cold, the flames burst out, burning all in sight. As the flames grew, the heat rapidly increased, melting people's soft skin. Brightness of colours blinded eyes and burnt all that it touched. The cold died, as I lit the fire, relaxing on the couch with a blanket.

Hannah Webster (14)
St Bede's RC Comprehensive School, Peterlee

Lost

As I jumped, the thought of falling was surging
through my head, but I didn't fall, I just floated there,
relaxed. I wasn't falling, there was no sound, if I
clicked my fingers, no sound. If I clapped, no sound.
What is this place? It was space! I was lost.

Christopher Renwick (14)
St Bede's RC Comprehensive School, Peterlee

The Weird Man

The dark so frightful, standing frail. He glared in the air, I shivered like a rocking chair in the wind. I ran. He was catching up. My nerves ran riot in my body. But, I heard a scream. I looked - it was a shot. There he was. He's dead!

Niall Brown (13)
St Bede's RC Comprehensive School, Peterlee

Untitled

The adrenaline was pumping, blood was rushing, life passed before me. What was happening to me? I was having optical illusions - a figure before my eyes. A faint voice from beyond …

'You are OK, don't worry. You have been in a very serious incident. You will soon be feeling better.'

Lucy Barnaby (13)
St Bede's RC Comprehensive School, Peterlee

251

The Landing

Another normal day started but that would change!
Me and my friends were walking in the town but
suddenly everything went black, light wasn't seen for
miles. Then a flash of light beamed on us; we were
blinded. The round object disappeared along with
what seemed like all the town!

Daniel Mearman (13)
St Bede's RC Comprehensive School, Peterlee

252

The Wacky Warrior

Bright lights flashed like diamonds before my eyes as I bounced from side to side in amazement. Lasers blitzed past my ears like bullets, the noise was unbelievable. I bounded around a little more, then rolled down the tunnel. When I fell out, I realised I was the *Pinball Wizard!*

Ryan Giblin (13)
St Bede's RC Comprehensive School, Peterlee

253

Chatted Into Flames

Delayed for twelve hours. Great! So much for my trip home. I sat alone for what seemed like ages, until an intellectual-looking man sat beside me. We introduced ourselves and chatted. Being really nice, I gave him my address as he left.
When I arrived home, flames surrounded me.

Sophie Garrett (13)
St Bede's RC Comprehensive School, Peterlee

Alleyways Are Bad News!

We met in an alleyway and started chatting. 'Nice
clothes,' I commented.
'Thanks,' he replied.
'I'm missing a sock and shoe,' I randomly complained.
'Shall I come round your house for a chat?'
'Yes.'
Later that night I awoke in the alleyway.
He had taken my box; now I'm homeless.

James Plunkett (13)
St Bede's RC Comprehensive School, Peterlee

Car Chase

As I drive in my car going faster and faster, being
chased by the coppers I start to get worried. I might
not make it past the border. Guns start firing at my
tyres as I see the border not so far away ... I cross
the border - it's not over.

Alex Robson (13)
St Bede's RC Comprehensive School, Peterlee

256

Untitled

Flying on its transparent gliders, soaring through the air, it brings fear to many and angers some, their weapon being paper. It sees its target, aiming for a girl's balloon. Zooming straight for the girl, landing its stinger into her arm.
And so the bee died, achieving its goal.

Gerard Thompson (14)
St Leonard's RC Comprehensive School, Durham

Let Go

Up came my hands. Ready for explosion. Old folk watching me on my own. The feeling got stronger, I clenched my eyes. I scrunched my nose. Opened up wide and that's when it happened. A sigh of relief. A blush of embarrassment. The sneeze was over!

Vicky Chamberlain (14)
St Leonard's RC Comprehensive School, Durham

Nervous Tick

'Tick-tock,' the clock speaks.
'Tap tap,' the ruler barks.
'Rip rip,' the paper screams.
As the door opens, I bite my nervous nails. The
silence is eternal. Only tick, tap and rip remain. All
look and stare at the opened door. Terrified, I pass.
The exams are over.

James Long (14)
St Leonard's RC Comprehensive School, Durham

259

Untitled

It glared at me through the glass. Every meal, every footsteps and even every trip to the toilet it would be there, haunting me. I'd had enough. We looked at each other and in a flash, I gripped its white, hairy body until it exploded.

My spot was gone.

Sophia Dellapina (14)
St Leonard's RC Comprehensive School, Durham

Hunter

It sits and stares at me with its huge beady eyes,
unwilling to move. I don't dare move in case it jumps.
I scream for help but nobody comes, so I decide I'll
have to risk it. I prepare to run. And *go!* The spider
sits, not bothered at all.

Rachel Mefia (14)
St Leonard's RC Comprehensive School, Durham

Darkness

With this I know all. I can see the world, a man eating
bees, a spaceship blasting off. But then, darkness.
What have you done? You took my knowledge, you
blinded my vision. Turn the TV back on. You can
hoover up later when I have gone.

Alexander Brown (14)
St Leonard's RC Comprehensive School, Durham

Untitled

The beggar woman knocks at the door with bouquets of bright fruit, asking for a coin or two in return. The twigs claw her face, entangling in her matted hair, scratching her worn face. A young woman with snow-white skin answers her call. Biting the fruit she falls: dead.

Alex Musto (14)
St Leonard's RC Comprehensive School, Durham

Peaceful Heights

Gripping on with every fibre of its being, struggling to stay alive, determined not to let nature win and kill yet another innocent creation. No use, it was all over. Swaying softly through the empty space beneath it until finally, the leaf lay with the other failed leaves.

David Gorfach (14)
St Leonard's RC Comprehensive School, Durham

264

Disappointment

I sat with my hands over my eyes. My insides whizzed round in a blender, causing a feeling of severe nausea. I dared to remove my hand for a split second, but couldn't bear to look. A cacophony of cries and cheers.

It's over, England are out, on penalties again …

Rebecca Quinn (14)
St Leonard's RC Comprehensive School, Durham

265

Untitled

Muscles freeze in horror. Eyes widen as the world is
cut off by sliding metal. Trapped. All sides closing in.
Knuckles whiten as desperate hands flail for safety.
The room becomes smaller and smaller. Suffocating.
Air becomes ice as the floor plummets downward.
It's over! Freedom. I've survived the elevator.

Francesca McLoughlin (14)
St Leonard's RC Comprehensive School, Durham

266

The End Of Life

I stood on the edge, waiting to take my final step. Blood rushing through my veins, my heartbeat in my head, my brain spinning, my willpower holding me up. I said goodbye to Mum in a note this morning. A voice sounds. It's time. Time to board the plane.

Danielle Page (14)
St Leonard's RC Comprehensive School, Durham

267

It's Now Or Never

The time is here. The time is now. I yell for help, no one can hear my pleas. He moves closer with his hairy, bare legs visible to the world. His large, beady eyes taunt me as I consider my next move. I leap for him, finally ... killed that spider.

Ashlee Coates (13)
St Leonard's RC Comprehensive School, Durham

Untitled

Twitching, unaware of how long it will take. How painful will it be? The cold metal point touches her skin. Sweat dripping down her face, tears streaming. When will it be over? Fists clenching tighter, biting her lip with fear. Do it! *Ping! Ping!* Two sparkling gems in her ears.

Jessica Forster (14)
St Leonard's RC Comprehensive School, Durham

269

Mash

I sat there staring at it, taking deep breaths before I began. Steam was rising from it. There was some sort of brown and steamy liquid which lay around the bottom of it. That was it. I began. I dug my fork into the mountain of mashed potato. Mmm … yummy!

Philippa Smith (13)
St Leonard's RC Comprehensive School, Durham

Best Friends

Abandoned, lonely, unwanted by my best friend.
Memories swarm from happy times spent together.
Why would she leave me? The embarrassment
embedded on her mind by her friends. Deserted.
Silence fills the air. Only her old best friends to talk
to. No one wants to be a rejected teddy bear.

Nadine Scuffy (14)
St Leonard's RC Comprehensive School, Durham

The Building

As I stood outside the dark grey building, my knees
quivered in terror at the sight. Iron bars clung to
the windows, turning an orangey colour. The huge
doors loomed and suddenly swung open, displaying a
maggot-crawling carpet and a bookshelf.
Then I walked into school.

Emily Tweddle (14)
St Leonard's RC Comprehensive School, Durham

272

Falcon

It swiftly took off into the air, using its strong wings to gently glide high over turning heads. The firm wind carelessly guided its flight among trees as it swooped downwards. It seemed to head back to the small crowd as a boy stepped out, grabbing his paper plane.

Wiff Lawrence (14)
St Leonard's RC Comprehensive School, Durham

Untitled

There was an anticipating wait that surrounded the classroom as the creature tormented us, flying around. Its smug appearance annoyed us all, the buzzing cries angered every pupil. As it made the naive mistake of landing on the desk, I had to decide in a heartbeat. I squashed the bee.

Conor Lavery (14)
St Leonard's RC Comprehensive School, Durham

Victory!

Heart pounding, arms pumping, muscles penetrating as I tore round the bend. Nothing was going to stop me now! It was in sight, that white line that separated me from sweet victory. I could no longer feel the breath of the other runners. I crossed the line, arms ablaze. *Victory!*

Godfrey Nyamugunduru (14)
St Leonard's RC Comprehensive School, Durham

The City

The bright lights, the taxis rushing by, all of the different sounds. That's just the first few things I love about the city. You're right in the middle of everything. You feel so involved. I walked into the new nightclub. *What could the big surprise be?* I wondered.

Bilgi Demirsöz (13)
Spennymoor Comprehensive School

Eleven Ghosts

It was a dark and foggy night. The house was empty and we drove away into the night towards my dreaded destination. I entered the creepy mansion. Suddenly someone or something came towards me from out of the darkness. Then all of a sudden, I was alone in the darkness.

Olivia Smart (11)
Spennymoor Comprehensive School

Night Of The Scorpion

A warm, silent desert, wind blowing, the red-chested
bird singing, humming tribe dancing cheerfully round
the sparkling fire, smelling burning. Ivory tents, loving
family sleeping.
Mum woke and gasped, sweating like a roasting pig.
The scorpion scattered - sharply escaping. Mum
knew life had just begun but now ended.

Alan Richardson (15)
Spennymoor Comprehensive School

Conor, Matty And Newcastle

'Very good skill, the both of you. Do you play for anyone?'

'Yes,' said Conor, 'we play for Byres Green.'

'OK, do you fancy playing for Newcastle?'

Straight away Matty said, 'Yes.'

Matty is Conor's best mate. Conor wasn't sure because he supported Sunderland, but eventually he said yes.

Conor Heaviside (12)

Spennymoor Comprehensive School

279

The Girl Who Nobody Knew

Sunny morning, she awoke and went downstairs. She flew through the door. Her mam looked at her as if she shouldn't be there. She was puzzled. 'Who are you?' she said.

'Your daughter,' she replied.

'What?' she screamed.

She went to ring her friend, who didn't know her either.

Jade Reiffy (12)
Spennymoor Comprehensive School

Flair

Flair was a boy who got picked on at school. Mostly it was the girls who picked on him; Flair wanted revenge on the girls and he got it. He threw mud at them and they never bullied him again, ever.

Lauren Cole Myers (12)
Spennymoor Comprehensive School

The Girl And The Shadow

On a hot night, I woke up very scared. I'd been having the same nightmares for days: about a shadow following me. I was sure I'd seen it before, while I was awake. I thought it was my dad behind me, but it wasn't. I looked everywhere … it *was* there.

Saysha Freeman (12)
Spennymoor Comprehensive School

Untitled

It was sports day at school. Lauren was running the 300m. Callum was running too. It was the final race and lots had been knocked out. They ran and Lauren won. Callum won as a runner-up.
'Well done!' shouted Miss Smart.
Lauren won £100.

Rachel Jenkins (12)
Spennymoor Comprehensive School

Information

We hope you have enjoyed reading this book - and that you will continue to enjoy it in the coming years.
If you like reading and writing, drop us a line or give us a call and we'll send you a free information pack. Alternatively visit our website at www.youngwriters.co.uk

Write to:
Young Writers Information,
Remus House,
Coltsfoot Drive,
Peterborough,
PE2 9JX
Tel: (01733) 890066
Email: youngwriters@forwardpress.co.uk